国家出版基金项目
NATIONAL PUBLICATION FOUNDATION

Planned by Zhuang Zhixiang   Edited by Pan Wenguo

READINGS OF CHINESE CULTURE SERIES
POETRY V
Selected *Ci*-Poems of the Song Dynasty

Compiled & Translated by Zhuo Zhenying

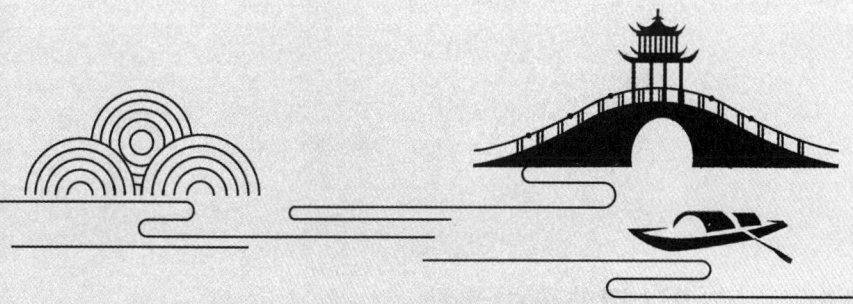

中国经典文化走向世界丛书

诗歌卷 五

庄智象◎总策划   潘文国◎总主编

卓振英◎编译

上海外语教育出版社
外教社 SHANGHAI FOREIGN LANGUAGE EDUCATION PRESS

www.sflep.com

图书在版编目(CIP)数据

中国经典文化走向世界丛书. 诗歌卷. 五/卓振英编译.
—上海：上海外语教育出版社，2018
ISBN 978-7-5446-5510-1

I. ①中… II. ①卓… III. ①中国文学—综合作品集—英文
②宋词—选集—英文 IV. ①I211

中国版本图书馆CIP数据核字(2018)第160681号

出版发行：**上海外语教育出版社**
       (上海外国语大学内)　邮编：**200083**
电　　话：021-65425300（总机）
电子邮箱：bookinfo@sflep.com.cn
网　　址：http://www.sflep.com
责任编辑：梁瀚杰

印　　刷：上海华业装璜印刷厂有限公司
开　　本：635×965　1/16　印张 5.75　字数 89千字
版　　次：2018 年 10 月第 1 版　2018 年 10 月第 1 次印刷
印　　数：1 100 册

书　　号：ISBN 978-7-5446-5510-1 / I
定　　价：**20.00 元**

本版图书如有印装质量问题，可向本社调换
质量服务热线：**4008-213-263**　电子邮箱：**editorial@sflep.com**

PREFACE

"Cherish one's own beauty, respect other's beauty, and when both beauties are respected and cherished, the world will become one", said Fei Xiaotong, a famous Chinese sociologist at a celebration party in honor of his eightieth birthday about thirty years ago. In a time of growing interest in intercultural communication today, these words sound especially wise and far-sighted. Translation, as one of the most important means for cultural communication, is usually done into one's mother tongue from other languages by native translators. This largely guarantees the quality of translated text, so far as the linguistic readability is concerned. However, this method implies a one-sidedness in correspondence, as only the translator's "respect for other's beauty" is concerned, regardless, though not completely, of how the local people look upon and cherish their own beauty. It should be compensated by translations on the other way, that is, works selected, interpreted, and translated by the local people themselves into languages other than their own. This approach may go directly against the prevalent views in modern translation theories but, in my opinion, is worthy of practicing. It is perhaps an even more effective way to bring about successful communication in cultures, and the beauties of the world can really be shared by the world's people. It is with such understanding that the Shanghai Foreign Language Education Press is organizing a new series of books, entitled *Readings of Chinese Culture*, to introduce Chinese culture, past and present, to the world, with works selected and translated by the Chinese scholars and translators.

The series will cover a wide range of writings including but not restricted to works of different literary genres. For the first batch, we are glad to provide three books of essays and one book of short stories, all written by authors of the 20th century. They will be continued by a batch of serious academic writings on premodern Chinese classics in philosophy, literature, and historiography, written by influential scholars of our time.

Later, we will offer more books on classical Chinese drama, classical Chinese poetry, etc.

Some of the books in the series have been published before, but they have been revised and rearranged for the new purpose to meet the current needs of broader readers. We are looking forward to hearing comments and suggestions on the series for future improvement.

Pan Wenguo

CONTENTS

INTRODUCTION

The founding of the Song Dynasty (960 – 1279) in the late 10th century ended the turbulent state of the Five Dynasties (907 – 960), restored social stability and revitalized the nation's economy, which allowed but did not necessarily ensure the prosperity of verse. For nearly forty years since the establishment of the empire, the world of poetry had been reigned by the frivolous Xikun School, which was given to the ornate representation of the leisurely and luxurious life of courtiers.

The Xikun School met its fate only after Ouyang Xiu and Mei Yaochen launched the Literary Reform Movement which, unlike the two political reforms respectively initiated by Fan Zhongyan together with Ouyang Xiu and by Wang Anshi, had turned out to be a great success. Ouyang, leader of the literary circle, and Mei, pioneer of Song poetry, stipulated that verse should mirror the reality and at the same time serve as a social corrective, and they pursued the aesthetics of simplicity, profundity and natural ease. The movement grew in strength with the participation of Wang Anshi and Su Shunqin, and it reached its zenith when the literary genius Su Shi, who played an important role in the development of *ci*-poetry, entered the poetical arena.

The *ci*-poetry is a verse form that had come into being in the Sui Dynasty and taken shape during the Tang Dynasty. It is also termed as "Song Words" or "Long-and-Short Lines". As the name suggests, the *ci*-poetry, more often than not, is verse of uneven line length originally set to music to be sung. The music has its tune names, and the words set to a particular tune follow a tonal pattern and rhyme scheme of their own. At first the *ci*-poetry had been exclusively devoted to romance subjects. Poets of the Sentimental School followed that tradition but assumed a more serious attitude towards topics of love than those of the Flower-Shade School of the Five Dynasties. Fan Zhongyan and Ouyang Xiu made successful attempts to open up new realms of thought, and Liu Yong diversified its form by creating "Long Tunes". On the foundation laid by his foregoers, Su Shi enlarged the conception of *ci*-poetry, sublimating it into a powerful instrument capable of expressing all kinds of sentiments and describing various walks of social life. Su's Powerful and Free School, which ushered in the golden age of *ci*-poetry, has produced a far-reaching impact on Chinese poetry and, in a broader sense, on Chinese literature.

The Literary Reform Movement split up after Su's death. Huang Tingjian and Chen Shidao founded the Jiangxi School, Zhou Bangyan pioneered the Metrical School, while Qin Guan and He Zhu flew their own colors.

In the early years of the Southern Song Dynasty (1127 – 1279), patriotism became a common theme of progressive literature. The poets of the Xin School, such as Lu You, Xin Qiji, Chen Liang, Liu Guo and Liu Kezhuang, represented the main stream of the Powerful and Free School. Their works are not only imbued with passionate patriotism, but they also present an irresistible aesthetic and artistic charm. Other important patriotic poets of the time were Yue Fei, Zhang Yuangan, Zhang Xiaoxiang, Fan Chengda and Yang Wanli. The great poetess Li Qingzhao and the famous poet Chen Yuyi, respectively representing the Sentimentalist and the Jiangxi Schools, had also taken part in the concerto of patriotism and struck touching notes.

The history of the Song Dynasty poetry was, as it were, brought to a solemn and stirring close by Wen Tianxiang, whose immortal poems "Song of Righteousness", "Crossing the Lonely Bay" and "Libation to the Moon over the Rill" (a *ci*-poem), like the excellent works of others, have an important bearing on the character of the Chinese nation.

Because of the unique charm in its artistic form, *ci*- poetry still boasts an irresistible appeal to contemporary poets and readers.

Chinese poetry is a great cultural heritage of all mankind. Unfortunately, appreciation of Chinese poetry is hindered by language and cultural barriers on the part of non-Chinese-speaking people, and the translation of verse is a real challenge. This notwithstanding, Chinese and foreign scholars have made laudable and fruitful efforts since the eighteenth century, though there is still something to be desired in the translations by and large.

Perhaps something more could be attained by standing on the shoulders of the giants before us? Perhaps the wonderful beauty of Chinese poetry could be preserved to the maximum in English translations? The answer should be in the affirmative, provided that we make assiduous and conscientious attempts.

The present collection is supposed to be one such attempt. Included in this collection are eighty oft-quoted *ci*-poems of the Song Dynasty, which are arranged in chronological sequence of the poets' births. Each piece bears a tune name, which might not be suggestive of the theme, and a "sub-title" (if there is one), which functions as the actual title. For the reader's reference, a note about the theme and/or style will be given to the tune name.

The Tower of Babel can be constructed only when people, scattered all over the world, have built up a perfect understanding among themselves. May this book facilitate the understanding and offer a small and yet useful brick for the construction of the Tower.

Zhuo Zhenying
October 1, 2007

The Southland in Spring[1]

◎ *Kou Zhun*[2]

Th' willows drooping low, the waters of yearning vast,
The village lonely, far and wide the grass extends.
At sunset apricot flowers fall thick and fast.
Spring over in th' south, my heart grief o'er separation rends.
Duckweed all o'er Tingzhou, would he return ere my bloom spends?

---

[1] This is the tune name of the *ci*-poem, as is the case with most of the poems included in the present collection. The present *ci*-poem expresses a young woman's yearning for her long-separated man with metaphoric language, which is apt to induce imagination.

[2] Kou Zhun (961 – 1023), courtesy name Pingzhong, had twice held the position of Prime Minister of the Northern Song Dynasty. His poetry features a sublime simplicity.

Pride of the Fisherman[①]

◎ *Fan Zhongyan*[②]

Th' frontier in autumn does present a scenery of its own,
But no signs of regret th' wild geese leaving for Hengyang have shown.
The bugle calling, horses neighing, th' winds now scream and now groan.
The sun drooping down perilous peaks, columns
Of smoke rising to th' sky, a town, with all its gates shut, stands lone.

A cup of wine drowns not nostalgia for home that's far away;
But ere my name's engrav'd in Mount Yanran, nothing'll me sway![③]
Frost is everywhere; melancholic strains the Qiang flutes do play.
What have th' countless sleepless nights been witnessing?
The frontier guards shedding tears, the general's hair turning gray.

---

① The present *ci*-poem describes the hardships of frontier life and expresses the soldiers' determination to defend their homeland in a vigorous style.

② Fan Zhongyan (989 – 1052), courtesy name Xiwen, a great statesman, philosopher, writer, educator, military strategist and philanthropist. "Be the first to handle the world's concerns as one's own and be the last to enjoy the world's benefits," a quotation from his famous essay *On the Yueyang Tower*, has been a maxim of millions.

③ This line means to say that nothing would sway the poet's determination before the invaders are swept away. The subordinate clause alludes to the heroic deed of General Du Xian of the Han Dynasty who, having defeated the invasion of the Huns in the A.D. 89, ascended Mount Yanran and had an account of the victory engraved on a rock.

Temple Music[①]

◎ *Fan Zhongyan*

Fleecy clouds drifting in th' skies blue,
Yellow leaves covering the land,
The waves are lent an autumn hue,
Over which a thin haze does expand.
The hills in the twilight, Earth and Heaven merge into one.
Flowers, unfeeling, are beyond the reach of th' setting sun.

So long from home I've been away
That nostalgia in me oft screams.
Awake at night I often stay,
Unless brought to sleep by soothing dreams.
If I lean alone on th' moon-lit railing, grief reappears;
And yet when I try to drown sadness, wine turns into tears![②]

---

① The present *ci*-poem expresses the grief over separation. Unlike poems of the similar themes, it is characteristic of a grandiose and vigorous total concept.
② The sentence "wine turns into tears" is a parable. On the surface the idea is absurd, and yet at the deep level it does make sense, for the poet's nostalgia is so keen that nothing could relieve it, and that wine would seem to turn into tears as soon as the poet drinks it.

Bells in the Rain

◎ *Liu Yong*[1]

Cicadas decrying the chill which befalls
In th' wake of the rain, the pavilion ahead
Bedims in the dusk as if it had a sorrowful heart.
The boat now relaying its urge in the calls,
At th' send-off out of the city in a shed,
Neither's in the mood for the wine, as I will soon depart.
We are full of tears but short of word;
We stand sobbing, eye to eye and hand in hand.
Destination lies far beyond the waves blurr'd,
Where the mist is hanging low o'er the southern land.

Love has been haunted by parting from of old,
Moreo'er I'm leaving on an autumn day so cold.
What shall I see when wine's effect weakens after the night?
Bank and willows under a pale setting moon — a strange sight.
I'll stay away for long long years, during which lovely days
And thrilling scenes would mean nothing to such a lonely heart.
Affections in me henceforward may seethe and burn and blaze,[2]
And yet to whom could I such tender sentiments impart?

---

[1] Liu Yong (987? – 1053?), courtesy name Qiqing, the first professional *ci*-poet. He diversified the form of *ci*-poetry by creating the "long tunes". Three of his representative works are included in this book. The present poem narrates the poet's sadness of parting with his love.

[2] The phrase "seethe and burn and blaze" constitutes a case of climax.

Watching the Sea Tide[①]

◎ *Liu Yong*

Th' center of th' Three Wu's and in th' Southeast a key place,
Qiantang has been known for its prosperity from of old.
Ten myriad homes, wealthy and poor, th' city does embrace,
And th' beauty of th' streets, willows and bridges is untold.
Th' Natural Moat flows to th' boundless great seas.
Both of its banks are fring'd with cloud-like trees,
And rolling up snow-like foam, th' roaring waves ahead surge.
Men to compete th' rich variety of luxuries urge.
The mansions with jewels and satins glare,
And silks and pearls are profuse at the fair.

The twin lake and th' undulating peaks in harmony lie.
In due time the late autumn osmanthus freshen the air,
And ten *li* of lotus in full bloom appeal to the eye.
Anglers chuckle here, and lotus-seed pickers giggle there.
Boatmen's ballads are heard in th' eve and Qiang Pipes in fine days.
The magistrate, escorted by hosts of riders, now sings in praise
Of th' rosy clouds, now stops to listen to flutes and drums with delight:
Someday he'll take the landscapes to th' Phoenix Pond to make a sight!

---

① This piece depicts the beauty and prosperity of Qiantang, i.e. now Hangzhou. The first stanza tells of
the long history and geographic importance of the city by presenting a bird's-eye view of it, and the
second stanza focuses on the narration of the majestic sights of the West Lake.

An Eight-Beat Song of Ganzhou^①

◎　*Liu Yong*

The evening rains are splattering over the stream,
Washing away autumn that's cool and clear;
The setting sun on th' tower does feebly gleam,
As the wind's chillier and th' landscape drear.
The red having faded, and wither'd the green,
Nature's breaths appear to have ceas'd,
Only the Yangtze River is seen
Meandering silently to th' east.

I can't bear to gawk far and on high stroll,
For when I gaze towards distant home,
Nostalgia will run out of control.
Alas! Whereat should I on strange lands roam?
Over recent years' drifting life I sigh!
How oft has my love on th' tower peer'd far away?
How oft has she taken th' returning sails
On th' horizon for mine? Oh, could she know that I,
Engrossed in a yearning dismay,
Am now leaning against the rails?^②

---

① *An Eight-Beat Song of Ganzhou*, regarded by Su Shi as "comparable to the best of the poetry of the Tang Dynasty in artistry", relates the nostalgia of the poet as a wanderer, which is set off by a vivid description of the bleak and dismal sights.
② In the form of a monologue, this stanza lays bare the keen yearning of the poet for his love and home.

Buddhist Dance①

◎ *Zhang Xian*②

On th' expressive *zheng*③ "Song of th' Xiangjiang Rill" she plays.
At first th' limpidity each note lively portrays,
Then in detail th' pent-up grief she does impart;
Her nimble fingers on th' thirteen strings dart —

Till the waters in front slow down for th' plight,
And wild geese from Jade Hill droop in their flight.
At last she strikes up the most plaintive strain,
When th' mountains seem to knit their brows for pain.

---

① The present piece describes the artistic realm the woman musician has attained: her plaintive strains are so fascinating that even the birds, hills and rills, personified, are deeply moved.
② Zhang Xian (990 – 1078), courtesy name Ziye, a poet famous for his exquisite lines.
③ A plucked instrument.

The Lily Magnolia[①]

◎ *Yan Shu*[②]

Swallows, wild geese and orioles in succession go. Helpless it seems!
Presumably in our fleeting life thousands of complexities lie.
How much longer are th' reunions with our dear ones than spring dreams?
And where can they be found when scattered like clouds in th' autumn sky?

Such ideal belles as Wenjun[③] and th' Goddess of Hangao[④] you cannot stay
When they're destin'd to go, e'en if a firm grip on their blouses you keep.
'Tis no use being solely sobre, and so keep in mind what I say:
It matters not if 'midst the flowers you take a drink and fall asleep!

---

① On the surface, the present *ci*-poem seems to express the poet's reflections on youth, companionship and life, which might be transient, and yet the interpretation might be misleading. As some critics hold, the poem gives vent to the poet's indignation over the demotion of the poet's political allies. In that case the poem may as well be regarded as a parable against the background briefed below: In the Reign of Qingli, the poet, in the position of Prime Minister, engaged himself in the political reforms in light of the ten countermeasures put forth by Fan Zhongyan, the then Deputy Prime Minister. When the empire began to show signs of progress, however, Emperor Renzong, who trusted in the opponents, removed the poet from office and sent the reformists out of the court. This *ci*-poem, in which the beauties embody the poet's talented allies, reflects the poet's disappointment of the throne and yearning for his political partners.

② Yan Shu (991 – 1055), courtesy name Tongshu, a statesman, poet and calligrapher of the Northern Song Dynasty.

③ Zhuo Wenjun (175 – 121 BC), the talented beauty of the Han Dynasty, fell in love with the famous writer Sima Xiangru for his enchanting music and literary gifts.

④ The legend goes that the Goddess of Hangao expresses her love for Zheng Jiaofu by giving him her jadeite pendant.

The Jade Tower in Spring[①]

◎ *Yan Shu*

The poplars, th' grass, and th' roadside shelter — everything still stays
Fresh in my mind, yet light of our parting he at th' time made.
Th' fifth watch sees me wake up from dreams and atop th' tower gaze,
And th' third month rains witness me seiz'd with grief in th' flower shade.

Th' unfeeling suffer less than the one whose heart with love pounds,
Of which an inch may contain a thousand strands and loose ends.
Even the sky has its limits and the earth has its bounds,
However, my lovesickness to infinity extends!

Rinsing Yarn in the Brook[②]

◎ *Yan Shu*

For each newly-writ song I drink a cup of wine,
In the same pavilion and weather as last year.
Would you e'er return? Alas, the sun's on th' decline!

In spite of my wish the flowers fall there and here;
Th' swallows, old friends as it were, are back. I alone
Pace on the garden's flower-fring'd path without cheer.

---

① This poem, in the pattern of a monologue, might express a young lady's lovesickness by means of contrast and metaphor. Controversially, the poet might intend to satirize the fatuous throne, which remains unfeeling in spite of the poet's high aspiration to contribute to his beloved nation.
② This poem, which relates the poet's longing for his friend, is suggestive of the philosophy that beauty, though seemingly absent sometimes, will remain in man's memory.

The Butterfly Fluttering around the Flowers[①]

◎ *Ouyang Xiu*[②]

Vast is the big courtyard. But how vast?
Poplars and willows stretch far like haze,
And screens and curtains are beyond cast.
Where's his jade bridle? Afar I gaze:
Tall as th' tower is, invisible Zhangtai[③] stays.

Late the third month, rains lash and winds rise.
As there is not a way to stay spring,
I have all gates clos'd. Tears in my eyes,
The plants to a talk I try to bring,
Which keep silent, their petals flying o'er the swing.

---

① The present piece deals with the theme of a lady's grievance over the long separation from her man. The description of the void of the courtyard in the first stanza serves to sets off the lady's disappointment, and the depiction of the elapsing spring in the second stanza symbolizes the shattering of her hope.
② Ouyang Xiu (1007 – 1072), courtesy name Yongshu and style name Old Drunkard, a statesman, historian, calligrapher, essayist and poet of the Northern Song Dynasty. He is one of the Eight Greatest Essayists of the Tang and Song Dynasties. His poems feature a fresh clarity.
③ In Chinese literature, the Zhangtai Road denotes the place wanderers frequent.

Hawthorns in the Wilderness[①]

◎ *Ouyang Xiu*

On th' eve of th' Lantern Festival last year,
The flower fair was lit up bright as noon.
We rendezvoused when dark night drew near
And o'er th' top of th' willows arose the moon.

Of this year's Lantern Festival on th' eve,
The moon and the lanterns remain as bright.[②]
But tears have wetted th' kerchief to my sleeve,
For my paramour is far out of sight.

---

① This poem reflects the poet's sincerity towards love. By picturing similar events on the similar occasions, it brings the happiness of the rendezvous and the separation-induced distress into a sharp contrast.

② The chain repetition of "Lantern Festival," "the moon," and "the lanterns" in this stanza reinforces the expressiveness of the poem.

Waves Washing the Sand[1]

◎ *Ouyang Xiu*

Proposing a toast to th' East Wind my cup I raise,
Wishing that she took her time and share'd the grace.
Along the willow-fringed road I lonely pace
To th' east of Luoyang[2], where we had toured before,
Feasting our eyes on peonies that we adore.

Caus'd by partings hasty and reunions brief,
There have been a thousand and one stories of grief.
Behold, the flowers are redder beyond belief
Than those of last year. Yet if next year's bloom does grow
Prettier still, with whom we will each come and go?

---

[1] The present piece expresses the poet's longing for his friend, who is believed by some scholars to be Mei Yaochen.
[2] Luoyang has been renowned for its peonies.

The Return of Ruan the Native[①]

◎ *Sima Guang*[②]

My fishing boat somehow haps to reach Dale Ever-Green,
O'er which to move at leisure th' sun and th' moon seem.
Charming is she, set off by th' carv'd window and gauze screen!
And our rendezvous is quite a perfect dream.

The morn dew's cold on pines, and th' clouds are thick in th' eve.
My oar ready, in haste I prepare to leave.
Now fallen flowers lie soundless and gurgles th' stream,
And to follow th' same route there 'tis hard, I deem.

---

① This tune name is derived from a legend, which goes as follows: Liu Chen and Ruan Zhao, who were from the now Zhejiang, went astray on their trip to Mount Tiantai to gather medical herbs. On a brook they met two belles, who offered to live together with them. When they returned half a year later, they found everything had changed and could see nobody they knew, for a period of seven generations had passed since they left. Is the present poem a poetic version of the legend, or is it mere reminiscence of the poet's romance? No definite answer is available at present.

② Sima Guang (1019 – 1086), courtesy name Junshi, a renowned writer and historian, who had held the position of Prime Minister. He authored the monumental history work *Zizhi Tongjian*, or *History as a Mirror for Governance*.

Fragrant Is the Cassia Twig[1]

◎ *Wang Anshi*[2]

Late autumn's chill felt in th' ancient capital, I gaze afar on high.
Th' thousand *li* River's like a ribbon; th' green peaks rise in clusters to th' sky.
Ships sailing in th' setting sun, th' wine shops' sign-flags in th' west wind,
   painted yachts,
Fleecy clouds, and egrets flushing from th' isles — all these do painting defy.

The bygone days had witnessed men vie for power and wealth and fame.
Besieg'd, th' monarchs still embrac'd their belles, and as a result disgrace came.
I sigh over th' rises and falls, of which history, as it were, makes game.
Only wither'd grass and mist are seen, gone are th' Six Dynasties for aye,
And yet the songstresses are still singing the captur'd king's song[3] today.

---

① The present piece expresses the poet's great concern about the fate of the nation. It begins by depicting the fascinating scenery of the city Jinling (now Nanjing), which touches off the poet's reflections on the history of the Six Dynasties.
② Wang Anshi (1021 – 1086), courtesy name Jiefu and style name Banshan Old Man, a statesman and poet, and one of the Eight Greatest Essayists of the Tang and Song Dynasties. He had been appointed Vice Prime Minister and Prime Minister in succession and had initiated the political reforms in the reign of Emperor Shenzong.
③ The song *Jadeite Trees in the Back Garden* is said to have been composed by the dissipated emperor of Chen (the last of the Southern Dynasties) for his favorite concubine before the loss of the empire.

The Jade Tower in Spring①

◎ *Yan Jidao*②

Once again the east wind is playing the mischief,
Sending to the ground flowers white and red and pink.
Tall walls and broad curtains by no means hide my grief,
As was the case with last year, when my heart did sink.

Though 'tis none of my business that spring'll elapse,
Sorrowful tears I shed whene'er I ascend heights.
In such a case I'll drink to my heart's content: p'rhaps
Before all the flowers fall, left are few delights.

---

① This poem, in which the east wind is personified, expresses the poet's sorrow over the elapsing spring.
② Yan Jidao (1038 – 1110), courtesy name Shuyuan, a poet well-known for his short *ci*-poems, which are characteristic of elegant language and tactful style.

Immortals over the River^①

◎ *Yan Jidao*

I wake up from dreams to find the tower lock'd;
When I'm sobered up, the curtains hang low there.
Last year at the elapse of spring I was shock'd:
Th' petals falling down, I stood alone in despair,
And pairs of swallows darted through th' drizzle in th' air.

Still fresh in my mind is how I first met Xiao Pin,
Whose silk blouse embroider'd with two hearts I did sight.
She express'd her love by plucking *pipa* from string
To string. At the time the moon was shining bright,
Which in th' end for the Rosy Cloud^② the way did light.

---

① This is the poet's representative work. It expresses the poet's longing for the songstress Xiao Pin in a
   simple and straightforward style.
② The Rosy Cloud, denoting the girl, is a case of metonymy.

The Diviner
To Bao Haoran, Who Is Leaving for Eastern Zhejiang[1]

◎ *Wang Guan*[2]

Th' waters clear are glances which from bright eyes flow,
And clusters of verdant mounts are brows rais'd high.
The traveler's destination do you care to know?
It is where the prettiest brows and eyes lie.

We have just sent off sweet Spring against our will,
And now farewell to you I will have to say.
If you chance to have the luck to meet Spring south of th' Rill,
Listen: as long as you can with th' season stay.

---

[1] This is the title of the *ci*-poem. As a rule, the title sheds light on the theme or purpose of the composition. As a send-off gift, the present poem wittily pictures nature as a beauty and expresses the poet's goodwill to his out-going friend. The language is metaphoric.

[2] Wang Guan (1035 – 1100), courtesy name Tongsou, a poet known for his freshness, jocularity and originality.

Buddhist Dance[1]

◎ *Wei Wan*[2]

The brook and th' hills set each other off 'gainst the setting sun,
Two love-birds flush up, for the steps atop th' tower them stun.
On th' brook's yonder side two or three houses lie;
Apricots flaming out o'er th' fences please th' eye.

Green poplars fringe the path that zigzags below
The bank, along which at dawn and dusk I go.
Now I have seen willow catkins fly three times,[3]
And yet the expected is still in strange climes!

---

[1] The present poem, of which the picturesque scenery tinctures the poem with a significant touch of light-heartedness, expresses a lady's yearning for her husband.
[2] Wei Wan, respectfully addressed Madam Wei, was a renowned poetess comparable to Li Qingzhao. Her husband Zeng Bu (1036 – 1107) was an ardent supporter of the political reforms launched by Wang Anshi.
[3] This is a roundabout way of saying "Now three years have passed."

21

Prelude to Melody of Flowing Waters

On the eve of the Mid-Autumn Festival of the Year Bingchen, I went on a night-long spree, and composed this piece when tipsy, with an intention to cherish the brotherly love for Ziyou.[1]

◎ *Su Shi*[2]

When did the brilliant moon come into being?
Raising my cup I ask the azure sky.
And what year's tonight in, I wonder, in light of
The calendar of the Palace on High?
The dread that it'd be too cold in the firmament
Gives me pause — otherwise riding on the zephyr
To the crystalline palace I would fly.[3]
And further: whom might I dance with up there but my shadow?
With this regard the fancy for celestial life seems wry.

Creeping from the other side of th' mansion,
Through the carv'd window on the sleepless
The moon mischievously casts its light.
Why should she ironically grow full when people part,

---

① This is an introduction to the *ci*-poem, which is one of the poet's masterpieces. It imparts to the reader the background, the theme and the purpose of the composition. The poet's brother Su Zhe, who is mentioned here as Ziyou (courtesy name), was also one of the Eight Greatest Essayists of the Tang and Song Dynasties. "As the moon may wax or wane and grow dim or bright, / So men thrive or decline and part or unite;" "Tis wish'd that we may all live in good health / And share — though far apart — the beauty of th' minor light!" These are among the oft-quoted lines, the former two lines to express consolation, and the latter two, good wishes.

② Su Shi (1037 – 1101), courtesy name Zizhan and style name Dongpo in Seclusion, was not only a leading figure of the Powerful and Free School of *ci*-poetry and an accomplished calligrapher, but also one of the Eight Greatest Essayists of the Tang and Song Dynasties. He had held the position of Minister of Rites and Education, and had encountered many a demotion. For details please refer to the Introduction.

③ The "crystalline palace" refers to "the Palace on High", where immortals are said to reside in light of the Chinese mythology.

As if upon men she were venting a spite?
Ay, but who can e'er change the course of nature?
As the moon may wax or wane and grow dim or bright,
So men thrive or decline and part or reunite.
'Tis only wish'd that we may all live in good health
And share — though far apart — the beauty of th' minor light.

The Riverside Town
Record of My Dream on the Night of the Twentieth
of the First Month of the Year Yimao[1]

◎ *Su Shi*

Alas! 'Tis been ten years since you did depart,
Over which grief has been gnawing at my heart.
You lie in the grave a thousand *li* away,
Without any means your loneliness to impart;
And I am so reduc'd as to give you a start —
Should we meet — my face dusty, and my hair frost-grey.

I dreamt I suddenly went home yesternight
And saw you making up at the table right
Behind th' window, that our tears roll'd down like threads
Of beads, and that we were both dumb because of th' plight.
Oh, I can tell how sad you are each year this night
On th' hillock, where on th' pines a wretched light th' moon sheds.

---

[1] The present *ci*-poem is an oft-quoted elegy, in which the poet expresses his keen and sincere love for his deceased wife in a straightforward style.

Charming Is Niannu
Reflections on Historical Events at the Red Cliff①

◎ *Su Shi*

The great River to the east surges high,
Washing th' fame of th' renown'd of yore away.
West to th' ancient fortress, th' Red Cliff does lie,
Where Zhou Yu② of th' Three Kingdoms, people say,
During the great campaign had made a name.
Lo, the jugged rocks are rising to th' skies,
And terrifying waves lashing on th' shore,
Rolling up a thousand piles of foam th' same
As snow. In a land fair as paradise,
How many of th' era are held in awe?

Tracing back to th' time of General Zhou,
Who, having just link'd a conjugal tie
To Xiao Qiao, with life and wit did o'erflow.
Feather fan in hand and in spirits high,
He had the foe's ships burnt to ash in th' stream.
One might jest that, so carri'd away
By th' historic site, my hair'll turn grey soon.
Oh, be soft now! Life's just like a brief dream.
In libation a cup of wine I may
As well offer from th' River to th' bright moon.

---

① This introduction lays bare the theme of the present masterpiece, of which the first stanza presents a grotesque picture of the ancient battlefield and the second extols the resourcefulness of the hero.
② Zhou Yu (175 – 210) was a general of the Kingdom of Wu, renowned for his resourcefulness.

The Butterfly Fluttering around the Flowers[1]

◎ *Su Shi*

Swallows darting, th' limpid stream does past th' house flow;
Flowers fading, unripe apricots are hanging green.
Fewer are willow catkins, for winds oft blow,
Yet everywhere fragrant grass and plants are seen!

On this side of th' fence th' passer-by is on his way,
And a maid giggles on the swing on the other side.
No more giggling's heard when footsteps fade away:
Alas, the dumb should have the loving defied!

---

[1] This *ci*-poem reveals the poet's optimistic attitude towards the elapsing spring. The first stanza pictures the beauty of nature by the end of the season, and the second describes whom the poet sees as a passer-by and how he feels about the chance encounter.

The Riverside Town
Hunting in Mizhou Prefecture①

◎ *Su Shi*

For th' moment to display the craze of th' young I'm bound:
Holding a falcon and the leash to a hound.
A thousand horsemen in hunting suits in th' wake
Come, sweeping across mountains and level ground.
I'll play th' part of Sun Quan②, a tiger shooter sound,
For the whole town pour out for the event's sake.

What matters if there are a few grey hairs on th' crest?
Reinforced by wine I feel at my best.
Oh, th' Feng Tang③ of today when will the throne send
As an envoy to reinstate the depress'd?
In time aiming my arrow at th' Wolf④ in th' northwest,
My bow into a full moon I shall bend!

---

① As an opponent to Sima Guang, the newly appointed Prime Minister, the poet was banished to Mizhou as the prefect. This poem, by narrating the hunting and alluding to a political event in the Han Dynasty, expresses the poet's aspiration to serve the nation by bringing his talent into full play.
② Sun Quan (182 – 252), the heroic King of Wu during the Three Kingdoms period.
③ This is an allusion to the history of the Han Dynasty. Wei Shang, prefect of Yunzhong, had been dismissed for a mistake in his report. Feng Tang, who talked Emperor Wen into remitting the punishment, was sent as an imperial envoy to the prefecture to reinstate Wei.
④ A star which symbolizes an invader in Chinese literature.

Yearning for the South
Composed at the Detachment Tower①

◎ *Su Shi*

Spring still in its prime,
Waving in the breeze are the willows trim.
To take a look the Detached Platform I climb:
Th' town's full of spring and th' trench is about to brim,
Though countless households th' mist and th' rain bedim.

After Cold Food Day②,
I sigh and lament when sobre from wine.
About old home to old friends you just nothing say,
To start a new fire and make new tea 'tis fine:
It is to youth that verse and wine incline.

---

① The poet came to Mizhou in the seventh year of the Xining Reign, i.e. 1074, and in the next year he
had an old tower renovated, which was renamed Detachment Tower by his younger brother Su Zhe.
This poem, which expresses the poet's homesickness, was written in the third year.
② The Cold Food Day, during which people stop cooking for three days, is observed in honor of Jie
Zitui, a sage of Jin in the Warring States period who declined the king's offer of enfeoffment to live
a secluded life. To scare him out from the mountains, the king had the trees burned, only to find the
sage dead in the fires. In grief, the king ordered that people stop cooking with fire for some time. The
festival begins two days before the Pure Brightness Festival.

Immortals over the River①

◎ *Su Shi*

Th' East Slope saw me drunk and sobre now and again,
When I came back 'twas around th' third watch or four.
Th' servant's thundering snores form'd an unbroken chain:
My knocks at the door he appear'd to ignore.
On my cane I went to listen to th' tide's roar.

That I can't be true to self 'tis a life-long shame,
When can I rid myself of worldly affairs?
Now that the night's deep, the weather calm and th' rill tame,
How I wish there were a little boat that bears
Me to the seas — and to a life free from cares!

---

① This *ci*-poem, which expresses the poet's disgust with the officialdom and longing for an unconstrained life, sheds light on the poet's optimistic broadmindedness.

Partridges in the Sky[①]

◎ *Su Shi*

Mounts clear on th' woods' verge, 'midst bamboos th' hut does lie;
Th' grass around th' pool languish, and cicadae yell.
From time to time white birds hover in the sky;
Th' scent of lotus flowers comes spell after spell.

From the huts to the ancient town, on my cane
I take a long walk at sunset at leisure.
Thanks to the mid-night rain I can once again
Enjoy, in my floating life, a day's pleasure.

---

① This *ci*-poem reflects the poet's optimistic adaption to his adversities. The employment of personification, the reduplicated words and the other techniques make the creation of images vividly unique.

Taming the Waves and Winds[1]

On 7th of the third moon, I was caught in rain on my way to Sandy Lake. As the rain-gear had been sent to the place in advance, all the company felt awkward except me. I composed this *ci*-poem when the rain stopped.

◎ *Su Shi*

What matters if on the woods and leaves splatters th' rain?
I may well recite poems while pacing on the cane
And in sandals, which than horseback make me more eas'd.
Howe'er could one with dread be seiz'd,
When his sanguine palm coat has brav'd life's wind and rain?[2]

I feel the chill when th' breezes sober me from wine,
But then a soothing sun atop the hill does shine.
I glance back at the place that I am to return:
There's th' seclusion for which I yearn:
'Tis secure and quiet, be th' weather rough or fine!

---

① The rain and sunshine in this *ci*-poem are respectively symbolic of the seamy and the bright sides of life, in face of which the poet, who has known the ups and downs, remains optimistically self-composed. The poem imparts to the reader the philosophy that one must not lose sight of the sunshine of hope in his adversities.

② These lines mean to say that, as he has experienced all sorts of sufferings and frustrations, the poet will remain dauntless in face of any kind of difficulties or dangers. In the phrase "his sanguine palm coat", the word "sanguine" is a transferred epithet.

Celebrating Peace and Order[1]

◎ *Huang Tingjian*[2]

Oh! Where is Spring?
I know not where to go in lonely dismay.
Would anyone who knows Spring's whereabouts kindly bring
Her word, requesting that she would with me stay?

Alas! Who knows, as no trace is to be found?
To seek th' oriole's advice I may well try.
Yet unfathomable's th' bird's twittering sound;
With a gust of wind o'er th' rose bush th' fowl does fly!

---

[1] This poem, with the overlapping events and images brought up in a natural graduation to a climax, expresses the poet's amorous thoughts of spring. In the poem spring is personified, and the oriole, which usually appears with spring, is symbolic of that season.

[2] Huang Tingjian (1045 – 1105), courtesy name Luzhi, was the founder of the Jiangxi School. He set store by the source of diction and the organization of composition. He was also a renowned artist and calligrapher.

Immortals on the Magpie Bridge[①]

◎ *Qin Guan*[②]

Her love into th' clouds the Maid subtly weaves,
And th' shooting stars display how th' Cowherd grieves.
When dew falls the Milky Way sees their meeting rare.
However, no secular love can e'er compare
With the holy sentiments they for a time share.

Their tender feeling is like a long stream;
Their rendezvous's like a transient dream.
They may not bear to part at th' Magpie Bridge! But nay,
So long as undying their affections will stay,
Whereat should they be bound up every night and day?

---

① This tune name derives from the myth of the love between the Cowherd (Niulang) and the Weaving Maid (Zhinü), who are separated by the Heavenly Queen with the Milky Way and allowed to meet only once in a year at the bridge built by the magpies which sympathize with them. The present *ci*-poem, a classic in the theme of the love story of the Cowherd and the Weaving Maid, vividly pictures the meeting of the two and expresses the poet's conception of love, which cherishes sincerity and sublimation. Employed are such devices as personification, simile and rhetorical question.

② Qin Guan (1049 – 1100), courtesy name Shaoyou and style name Huaihai in Seclusion, had been Collator at the Commission of Classics and Documents and Compiler at the Institute of National History before he was banished to Chenzhou and Leizhou in succession. He was a prominent poet known for his graceful elaboration and moderate richness.

Walking on Grassland[1]

◎ *Qin Guan*

Towers lost in th' mist of a plight,
The ferry vague in a moon that looks pale,
The Dale of Peach Blossom[2] is out of sight.
In th' lonely inn spring cold does me assail;
At dusk to th' setting sun th' cuckoo does wail.

The silk scrolls stuck in th' fish bellies
And all the flowers sent by post[3], oh lo!
Pile up tall as my countless grievances.
Th' Chenjiang Rill round th' Chenshan Hill ought to go:
Why does it to th' Xiao and th' Xiang Rivers flow?

---

① This *ci*-poem was possibly written in the spring of 1097, when the poet was banished to Chenzhou, a place bleak and desolate at the time. The mist, the assailing chill, the pale moon and the cuckoo's wailing mentioned in the poem are symbolic of setbacks and hopelessness, and the rill flowing elsewhere metaphorically denotes the frustration of the poet's aspiration to render service to the nation.

② This is an allusion to Tao Yuanming's namesake essay, meaning the ideal land (roughly equivalent to Utopia).

③ The silk scrolls stuck in the fish bellies / And all the flowers sent by post: These lines contain two cases of metonymy denoting "messages" or "letters".

The Half-dead Parasol

(Also Named "Yearning for the Yues" or "Partridges in the Sky")[1]

◎ *He Zhu*[2]

Reentering th' Changmen Gate, everything changed I find;
Since we'd shar'd life, why not share it through? Why leave me behind
Like a Chinese parasol half dead after hoary frost,
Or a lone white-hair'd mandarin duck flapping with th' mate lost?[3]

The grasses on the plain must still be wet with dew at dawn?
'Tis for you in th' new grave that I in th' old nest always mourn.[4]
Listening to th' pelting rain I groan on th' half-vacant bed:
Whoever could mend my coat in the lamplight in your stead?[5]

---

[1] As one of the best elegies in *ci*-poetry, the present piece, written in memory of the poet's deceased wife, ranks as high as Su Shi's *The Riverside Town* in artistry as well as in popularity.

[2] He Zhu (1052 – 1125), courtesy name Fanghui, a versatile poet. His compositions are characteristic of an exquisite diction and a varied style.

[3] The rhetorical questions, seemingly irrational, serve to give an emphatic effect to the expression of the poet's heart-rending grief; and apt are the cases of simile, which liken the poet to a half-dead parasol and a lone white-haired mandarin duck.

[4] The word "nest", logically in concert with the "lone mandarin duck", is a case of metaphor denoting "home".

[5] Ingenuous is the creation of the image of the poet's wife mending a coat for the poet in the lamplight, for the act is typical of wifely care and, in addition, the image is, as it were, spotlighted.

Life Journey Is Full of Perils

(Petty Plum Flowers)[1]

◎ *He Zhu*

I have two tiger-taming hands and an eloquent tongue, though,
In a coop-like carriage drawn by th' dog-like horse I'll go
To th' capital. I shall prove I'm no mediocrity,
Though my headband now suggests of no post and dignity.
The magnolias taken off their bloom, with th' folks I part
For Xianyang, o'er which Heaven'd get old if it had a heart.
Like Lei the Crazy[2] wealth I'll make light. About price who'd care?
Even ten thousand taels for a *dou* of wine I won't spare!

For th' sake of life to a large wine-cup I will henceforth hold:
Whose temple hair has remain'd raven for e'er from of old?
By the way, in watching performances there is no harm:
The girls' smiles and dances and silver tongues exude with charm.
Song to Autumn's fresh in our minds, but a thousand years have pass'd
Since it was compos'd. Isn't life transient? And isn't time too fast?
With this regard I'd tie the sun to Fusang Tree[3] with beams of light.
Howe'er, I'd find a day too long to bear when in a wretched plight.[4]

---

① The tune name, unlike those of the other pieces, is suggestive of the theme: the poet's burning indignation over the social reality, in which life's journey is full of perils and a gifted man can find no scope for his rare abilities. In this poem, allusions (such as that of "no mediocrity" to Li Bai) are aptly employed.
② This refers to Lei Yi of the Han Dynasty, who was known for his strong sense of justice and readiness to help the weak. He had helped a person get remitted of his punishment but refused to accept his gold gift, and declined the offer of an official position by pretending to be mad.
③ According to Chinese mythology, the sun rises from Fusang Tree.
④ The contrast formed by the conception of time being too fast and that of "a day too long to bear", reveals the poet's inner contradiction, which serves as a foil to the poet's frustration.

Rinsing Yarn in the Brook[①]

◎ *He Zhu*

The idea that sweet spring hates the aged I doubt:
How many springs ahead can the aged enjoy?
One can't be too frequent in spring to roam about!

In laughs and songs I behave like a naïve boy.
As one is absolutely honest when he gets drunk,
Feasting on th' wine and th' bloom I defy conducts coy!

---

① In the present *ci*-poem, by laying bare his viewpoint upon spring and, in a broader sense, upon life, the poet expresses his love for honesty and disgust with hypocrisy. The first stanza involves the catchword repetition of "spring", and the second stanza, a case of simile.

The Butterfly Fluttering around the Flowers①

◎ *Zhou Bangyan*②

The moon drear, the startled crows seem unrest;
Dawn breaking, the whining of th' well-pulley one can hear.
Rous'd, my sweetheart appears bright-ey'd and distress'd.
Alas, her pillow is wet and cold with tear!

She holds my hand in hers, reluctant to part;
Her temple hair floating in th' frosty wind, every word
She utters before leaving gnaws at my heart.
Oh, th' soul's out of sight, only cocks' crows are heard!

---

① The present *ci*-poem, by describing in detail the parting of the man and his sweet, manifests the keen affections between the two.
② Zhou Bangyan (1056 – 1121), courtesy name Meicheng and style name Qingzhen in Seclusion, was a prominent figure of the Sentimental School. He had served as an official at the Imperial Institute of Dasheng, which took charge of musical affairs, and had contributed a great deal to the development of *ci*-poetry. His compositions are elegant in diction, meticulous in meter and neat in organization.

Temple Music[①]

◎ *Zhou Bangyan*

Eaglewood is burn'd to dispel
Moisture; Th' peeping birds from the eaves
Twitter of a fine day to tell.
In th' morning sun th' raindrops on th' lotus leaves
Shrink, which, green and round on the surface, do appear
To be held high above the waters clean and clear.

My hometown is far far away!
Oh, whenever can I return?
Why should a native of Wu[②] stay
Long in Chang'an[③]? Ah, do th' fishermen yearn
For me too? I oft go to them in my sweet dream:
In a swift boat I row to Lotus Pool down th' stream!

---

① Unlike many of the poet's compositions, this *ci*-poem, which features a natural ease and simplicity, is free from elaboration. In the first stanza, the overlapping images of twittering birds, the rising sun, the rain drops on the green lotus leaves, etc., presents a word picture of the summer morning; while in the second, which involves the employment of rhetorical questions, the poet expresses his homesickness and yearning for the friends in his distant hometown.

② Now Jiangsu.

③ Chang'an had been the capital of the Tang Dynasty. Here it is a metonymy referring to Bianjing (now Kaifeng), capital of the Northern Song Dynasty.

Yu the Beauty[1]

Composed under the Blooming Crabapple Tree, When I Arranged a Drink
with Ganyu and Caiqing after the Rain

◎ *Ye Mengde*[2]

Yestereve the petals danced under th' wind's shake,
And rain arrived in their wake.
At dawn left in the yard was just half of the bloom,
While in th' clear sky a myriad *zhang*[3] of homesickness seem'd to loom.

We hold each other's hands under th' crabapple tree;
Our cups refill'd , we go on th' spree.
When th' banquet comes to an end, e'en th' maids their brows knit,
Let alone me, the helpless host who is more than affectionate!

---

① As the critics have commented, the poet pictures tender affections with a vigorous hand in the present
poem.
② Ye Mengde (1077 – 1148), courtesy name Shaoyun and style name Shilin in Seclusion, had held such
positions as Prefect of Jiankang, Minister of Personnel, etc. He was also a famous prolific writer. So
far as his style of *ci*-poetry is concerned, he had been a Sentimentalist who turned to the Powerful and
Free School.
③ A unit of Chinese measurement equaling ten *chi*.

A Blessing at Hand[1]

◎ *Zhu Dunru*[2]

After a shake I've cast off th' shackles of worldliness,
And now at my own sweet will I get drunk, or sobre grow.
I love my bamboo hat, my palm-coat and my business,
And more oft than not I tread the frost and brave the snow.

Th' wind calm at dusk, my fishing line resumes its serenity;
Either in th' skies or waters is seen a new moon bright.
Boundless waters and skies merging into an entity,
A lonely wild goose is now in sight, now out of sight.[3]

---

[1] This is one of the poet's six *ci*-poems on the theme of a fisherman's life. Zhu's poetry features an original conception and a vigorous and natural style.

[2] Zhu Dunru (1081 – 1159), courtesy name Xizhen and style name Yanhe, had lived a secluded life before he held the post of Proofreader at the Imperial Commission of Classics and Documents. Having experienced the ups and downs, he left the court in 1149 and lived a retired life in today's Jiaxing, Zhejiang.

[3] The image of the wild goose is symbolic of freedom.

Yanshan Pavilion[①]
Composed at the Sight of Apricot Flowers on My Way North

◎ *Zhao Ji*[②]

Ice-like gauze tailored with a rare grace
And deftly folded is your costume,
And lightly made up with rouge is your face.
What fascinating looks you assume!
In beauty the fairies you outshine,
Besides, you shed a comforting perfume.
However, you are prone to away pine,
In addition, ruthless are the rain
And th' wind, which deprive you of days fine.
What grief and pain!
Confined to the desolate yard,
How much more suffering must you sustain?

My boundless sorrow who could convey?
The pair of swallows, which here fly,
May not understand what I have to say.
Besides, the former palaces lie
Beyond a thousand mountains and streams.
Their senses th' complexity may defy.
Oh, court life's gone for aye except in dreams!
I can't cease to miss it and sigh.
Absurd it seems
That these days it ne'er occurs e'en if asleep I lie!

---

① This poem, written on the northward journey of the poet as a prisoner-of-war, expresses the poet's deep sorrow over the fall of the capital and the defeat of his empire. In the first stanza, the beautiful flower symbolizes the poet, and the winds and rains, the ferocious invading foes; and in the second stanza, in which such cases as hyperbole and rhetorical question are involved, the poet gives vent to his depression by means of recalling his former life and manifesting his moods.

② Zhao Ji (1082 – 1135), or Emperor Huizong of the Song Dynasty, was a talented painter, calligrapher and poet. After Song's defeat by the Jin forces, he and the royal family were taken captive in 1127. He was sent to the Jin region in the north, where he died in captivity.

Liuyao Melody[①]

Reflections on History (Improvised at the Banquet on Poyang Lake in
Reply to He Fanghui in the Same Rhyme Sequence)

◎ *Li Gang*[②]

The thousand-*li* Yangtze River lies
Long and vast in th' haze, and its waves roll.
"Trees of Jade"[③] has been rais'd to the skies,
Just the bells from th' temples in time toll.
How time flies! The rises and falls, it seems,
Of Six Dynasties were but transient dreams.
The flames of war were gone for aye,
And sumptuousness didn't long stay,
But th' moon still waxes and wanes in its own way.

Th' waters boundless, th' tide ebbs and flows, and behold,
The riverside trees are as dense as hair.
Who could have thought that I should have return'd old
And dismiss'd, having fallen into th' snare?
E'en if the way is long and the times are hard,
My pursuit of th' goal nothing can retard.
On the top of the tall tower I lean
Against the railing, as to gaze afar I'm keen,
When braving th' snow o'er th' rill a fearless angler's seen[④].

---

① The present *ci*-poem, through reflections on history, expresses the poet's firm belief in the policy of
armed resistance, a policy in opposition to the policy of peaceful settlement. The other poet present
on the occasion was He Zhu, who is mentioned in the introductory remarks as He Fanghui (courtesy
name).

② Li Gang (1083 – 1140), courtesy name Boji, was a renowned statesman. He had held such positions
as Deputy Minister of Defense and Prime Minister. His poetry, overflowing with patriotism and
humanism, is characteristic of realistic charm.

③ *Jade Trees on the Backyard* (*Jade Trees* for short) is the name of a poem, which was set to music of the
namesake. It was composed by Chen Shubao, the last emperor of the Southern Dynasties who
fatuously indulged himself in pleasures.

④ An angler braving the snow over the river is the image of a fearless reformist created by Liu Zongyuan
(773 – 819) in his poem *The River Permeated with Snow*.

Beats Slowing Down①

◎ *Li Qingzhao*②

Fumbling and searching, at a loss I feel,
At a loss in such lonely melancholy
And plaintive solitude as seem unreal.
Th' turn of cold and warmth is, incredibly,
The most miserable time to endure.
Of th' chill of morning winds how can I cure
Myself with a few cups of wine impure?
'Tis heart-rending to see th' wild geese③ in th' sky —
My acquaintances of old — southward fly!

Chrysanthemums now flourish here and there,
But who would care to pluck them, feeling blue?
Sitting alone at th' window in despair,
Ere night falls I know not how to pull through.
Now dripping and dropping incessantly
On the Chinese parasols is the rain.
Alas, much much more than anxiety,
At such a time, is what one must sustain!

---

① As it is of slow beats and sounds plaintive, the tune suits such themes as departure, loneliness, misfortunes, etc. The present *ci*-poem, beings a case in point, expresses the poetess's deep sorrow over the adversities inflicted by the invading Jin forces. The repetition of "at a loss", the device of climax, and the moodiness built up in intensity by the expressions "at a loss" and "in such lonely melancholy and plaintive solitude as seem unreal", make the poem touching.
② Li Qingzhao (1084 – circa 1155), style name Yi'an in Seclusion, has been acknowledged as the greatest poetess in Chinese literature. Though a representative of the Sentimental School, she sometimes sounds powerful and free, especially when she touches upon such themes as of patriotism, courage and the significance of life.
③ The wild goose is an image suggestive of "home" or "message" in Chinese literature. It is derived from a knit-up tale for the rescue of Su Wu (140 – 60), an envoy from the Empire of Han who had been detained by the Huns for ten years.

43

Tipsy in the Shade of Flowers①

◎ *Li Qingzhao*

Mist follow'd by dark clouds, I have been sad all day,
Watching the incense in th' censer burning away.
The Double Ninth Festival② has now come again,
Yet in th' gauze screens and on th' jade pillow I up stay,
Feeling at midnight th' chilly loneliness and pain.

'Midst chrysanthemums I took a drop in the eve,
Which have left a puff of light fragrance in each sleeve.
That lovesickness is not consuming who can say?③
When it rolls up the curtain, the west wind would grieve
At a figure thinner than the flower today.

---

① In the present *ci*-poem, the poetess expresses her yearning for her husband Zhao Mingcheng, an epigraphist. The style is simple and natural.
② The festival, which reminds people of filial piety and keeping fit, is observed on the ninth day of the ninth lunar month, on which people will take a taste of chrysanthemum wine, wear a twig of the plant called *zhuyu* (i.e. fructus corni) and go mountaineering.
③ This rhetorical question means that lovesickness is undoubtedly consuming.

A Dreamy Strain①

◎ *Li Qingzhao*

The rain was light but the wind fierce yestereve;
Wine's effect on me my sound sleep didn't relieve.
I ask about th' begonias on which I'm keen.
"They're as nice as before," says the maid, rolling up th' screen.
"Do you know?
Do you know?"
Retort I, "What's red should be paler than what's green."

---

① The present *ci*-poem expresses the poetess's love of and sympathy for what is beautiful, which is ruined by the vicious forces incarnated by the winds and rains. Expressive is the movie-like dialogue, which is foreshadowed by the first two lines.

In Memory of the Belle of Qin①

◎ *Li Qingzhao*

Atop th' tower I gaze
At the hills disarrayed and th' plain wrapped in haze.
In the haze②
Th' crows return to their nests
At dusk and the horns craze.

My moods bad, of th' incense burnt out or broken I pall;
Under the urge of the west wind parasol leaves fall,
The leaves fall,
Ushering in autumn
And solitude and all.

---

① The defeat of the Song forces and the loss of territories had reduced the poetess to a homeless wanderer. In her mind's eye the haze-shrouded land has been shattered into pieces, and the falling leaves, the crows and the horns are just foretelling solitude and wretchedness and everything.
② The catchword repetition of "In the haze" is in concordance with the metrical rule of this *ci*-poem, and so is the case with that of "The leaves fall" in the next stanza.

A Twig of Plum Flowers[1]

◎ *Li Qingzhao*

Th' mat's chill, and autumn's taken off th' lotus' bloom;
Intending to chase away my gloom,
I go alone on deck th' orchid yacht.
When back, I ascend th' moon-lit tower, to spot
The wild geese[2] flying over the skies
Without bringing me a great surprise!

The petals drift and th' stream flows in their own way.
Though in different places we stay,
The same ardent affections we share.
From such feelings you just can not away tear:
For whenever from the brows they part,
They all at once come into the heart.

---

[1] This *ci*-poem expresses the poetess's keen yearning for her husband. The first stanza narrates the loneliness in the separation, and the second vividly likens the mutual affections to something visible and alive.
[2] In Chinese literature, the wild goose embodies the messenger.

Pride of the Fisherman[1]

◎ *Li Qingzhao*

Th' cloud-like waves and th' morning haze merge in th' sky;
The sails dance and th' Milky Way whirls on high,
In a dream to the Providence I fly.
"Please let me know,"
He amiably says, "where you will go."

"Long long is th' way and th' sun is on th' decline,"
I reply, "What if my poetry is fine?
Since th' Roc'll fly nine myriad *li* and nine[2],
Would you ask th' blow
To send my boat to th' Three Isles[3] at a go?"

---

[1] Soaring imagination marks the present *ci*-poem. Unlike many of the poetess's other pieces which may sound sentimental, it is free and powerful in style. The first stanza unfolds a magnificent picture of the poetess touring the universe, and the second, in which allusions to Qu Yuan, Zhuangzi and the legend about the immortals are employed, expresses the poetess's disappointment with the reality and aspiration to further sublimate herself.

[2] In light of Zhuangzi's fable, the Roc is capable of covering a very long distance.

[3] The Three Isles refer to the Isles of Penglai, Fangzhang and Yingzhou, believed to be the abodes of immortals.

The Lily Magnolia[1]
(A Simplified Version)

◎ *Li Qingzhao*

From the peddler I choose and buy
A spray of flowers that's alive with spring hue.
It gleams with tear[2] that's not yet dry —
And th' tinctures of rosy clouds and morning dew.

For fear my lover might not grant
That as the flowers my features are as fair,
I wear it on th' temple on th' slant
To make it easier for him to compare!

---

① This *ci*-poem, by drawing a word picture, so to speak, of a lovely spray of flowers and a lively girl, lays
   bare the inner world of the girl, which is active with ardent love for the soul of her heart. The language
   is simple but expressive, and the style glows with a natural ease.
② Here the morning dew is likened to tear — tear of happiness or excitement rather than that of sadness.

Spring in Wuling①

◎ *Li Qingzhao*

Th' wind subsides, dust smelling of fallen flowers here and there;
Th' sun's high up, but I can find no mood to comb my hair.
Gone is everything with my man, though his things still remain.
Before I can utter a word down roll tears of pain!

It is said that in Twin Rill there is no lack of spring scene,
I'm kind of stirr'd up to canoeing on which I'm keen.
However, I doubt if there is a boat big enough there
That can bear the weight of so much sorrow and despair!②

---

① In 1127, the Jin forces swooped south. To escape from the flames of war, the poetess fled to the south with her husband. After her husband died of illness in Jiankang (now Nanjing), she was reduced to wandering from Lin'an (now Hangzhou) to Yuezhou (now Shaoxing) and then to Jinhua. In the present poem, which was written during the poetess's stay in Jinhua, the poetess expresses her deep sorrow over her husband's death and the heart-rending loneliness that she has to endure.

② The expression "the weight of so much sorrow and despair", which ingenuously and implicitly likens "sorrow and despair" to something visible and weighty, constitutes a case of synecdoche.

Pride of the Fisherman[1]
An Inscription on the Portrait of Zhang Zhihe[2]

◎ *Zhang Yuangan*[3]

Clouds fleeting o'erhead, in a palm-coat you sail in the rill
In spring, which is wall'd on both sides with many a green hill.
When the white birds hover around, your cabin the winds fill.
Lo, the fishing line is pull'd up!
Yutong th' boy claps his hands and Qiaoqing th' maid with laughs does thrill.

The bright moon in the great void on all men alike has shone.
In your floating life you ignore whether it's dusk or dawn.
You love wine, but clamorous city life you hold in scorn.
While th' mist and waves are at their best,
Who could afford from th' racketing world to invite a thorn?

---

[1] This *ci*-poem, by depicting the unfettered life of Zhang Zhihe, lays bare the poet's disgust with worldliness and love for freedom and independence.
[2] Zhang Zhihe (circa 732 – 774), who mainly led a secluded life, was a famous poet and artist of the Tang Dynasty.
[3] Zhang Yuangan (1091 – circa 1161), courtesy name Zhongzong, was a pioneer of the Xin School. He served under General Li Gang as a non-military clerk.

The River All Red①

◎ *Yue Fei*②

I lean on the railing, bristling in righteous wrath,
The spattering rain beginning to withdraw.
With pent-up aspirations seething in me,
I gaze afar and skyward roar.
Rank and merit achiev'd at thirty years are but worthless dust;
An eight-thousand-*li* expedition's like the moon I adore!
Waste not my youth, for if my raven hair for nothing turn'd grey,
Grief and regret would my heart gnaw.

We've not yet aveng'd th' Humiliation
Of Jingkang③ upon the enemies;
Howe'er can we officials to the crown
Our burning indignation appease?
Riding on chariots over Mount Helan,
Enemy forts we'll crush and seize.
We are pledg'd to hungrily feed on the foreign invaders,
And, as if thirsty, with th' blood of th' Hun steeds we'll go on sprees,
Until we have recover'd our sacred territories,
When we can be present at Court at ease.

---

① This *ci*-poem, in which the poet expresses his ardent love for his nation, his bitter hatred for the invaders and his firm resolution to recover lost territories, is a classic in patriotic themes. It has been a great encouragement to the Chinese people in times of foreign aggressions.
② Yue Fei (1103 – 1142), courtesy name Pengju, was a general renowned for his armed resistance against the aggression of the Jin forces. He had held the position of Deputy Minister of Defense. As he was opposed to the capitulatory policies, he was ensnared by the Prime Minister Qin Hui and put to death. He remains an immortal national hero whose stirring patriotism will forever glow with glory.
③ The Humiliation of Jingkang refers to the Song Dynasty's defeat in 1127 by the northern Jin forces, which conquered the Song capital Bianjing and captured the Song emperors Qinzong and Huizong.

The Butterfly Fluttering around the Flowers①
Farewell, Spring!

◎ *Zhu Shuzhen*②

Beyond the tower th' weeping willows reach out
Countless twigs, intending to hold up Spring, which soon flees.
Th' trees, as if curious of Spring's whereabout,
Send out their catkins to follow close the breeze.

From the green hills come the cuckoo's plaintive cry:
If th' bird were unfeeling, why does it wail o'er man's pain?
Cup in hand I pledge Spring, which gives no reply,
When swashing and splashing down comes th' evening rain.

---

① This is an expression of sadness over the elapsing spring, but the poetess's light-heartedness is unique. The technique of personification makes the poem fresh and vivid.
② Zhu Shuzhen (1135 – 1180), style name The Secluded, was a poetess whose talent is only next to that of Li Qingzhao.

Charming Eyes①

◎ *Zhu Shuzhen*

A faint fragrance drifts along the flower-fring'd path in th' air;
The sun shining, th' breeze caresses th' willows with care.
After Pure Brightness I can't bear,
However, to recall the days of th' past,
When with dark clouds the tower's overcast.

The melodious voices of warblers, which to my ear
Sound like cries of grief after my noon nap, appear
To be coming from far and near —
From th' willows green, from th' apricots in red,
And from th' begonias beside the shed.

---

① Through the description of spring-induced grief, which permeates the premises, the poem reflects the poetess's sorrow caused by her unfortunate marriage. The vividness might be attributed to such devices as personification and parallelism.

Partridges in the Sky[①]

◎ *Lu You*[②]

In th' greenish mist and soft sunset rests my home,
Which from the dust of worldly affairs is free.
Th' nectar sipped, 'midst the bamboo groves I roam;
Th' Buddhist Scripture clos'd, I watch the mounts with glee.

I love reciting poems; 'bout mishaps who'd care?
Amuse myself here and there as well I may.
Creator has a varied heart, I'm aware,
To which it's nothing to let heroes decay.

① In 1166, after he was removed from office as Deputy Prefect of Longxing, the poet began to lead a secluded life on the Jinghu Lake (in other words the Mirror Lake), where the present poem was written. The poem pictures a secluded life and a lofty detachment from the social reality, to which the poet appears to be inclined; however, the last two lines reveal the poet's actual state of mind — not that the poet is cynical, but that he is indignant, for he could find no room to bring his talent into full play.

② Lu You (1125 – 1210), courtesy name Wuguan and style name Fangweng (i.e. the Unconstrained), had in succession held administrative positions and served in the army under the command of Wang Yan. As he was in conflict with the capitulatory clique, he was removed from office. In the reign of Emperor Ningzong, he became editor-in-chief of the Imperial Library. Afterwards he lived a secluded life in his hometown Shanyin (now Shaoxing, Zhejiang). Lu loved peace, hated unjust wars, and sympathized with the suffering millions. His poetry glows with humanism.

55

Partridges in the Sky[①]

◎ *Lu You*

The melon grower of the Green Gate[②] who cares
To copy? In fishing I shall find delight.
The swallows dart about the spring banks in pairs,
And hosts of gulls on the evening sand alight.

The oars creaking, songs are resounding in th' air,
Th' dishes seem to bloom, and as dew th' wine is clear.
Smiling and pointing to the boat, when ask'd where
I shall return, I'll reply: "I live right here!"

① The present *ci*-poem expresses the poet's enjoyment of an unfettered life and pride of being a fisherman free of worldly cares and desires.
② This alludes to Shao Ping of the Han Dynasty, who made a name by growing melons outside the Green Gate of the capital.

Phoenix Hairpin[1]

◎ *Lu You*

Reaching out her pinkish delicate hand,
She pour'd wine with a seal of famous brand;
We enjoy'd a parkful of spring where willows green did stand.
But alas, th' hateful East Wind play'd th' mischief;
Harmonious conjugal life was cut brief.
A few years of cruel separation[2]
Has made our hearts aching without relief.
What grief, grief, grief!

Spring, as usual, now has come again,
However both have grown haggard in vain,
The satin handkerchief being wet with tears of great pain.
Peach flowers now fall down throng after throng,
Th' ponds and pavilions desolate for long.
Although to oaths we'll for aye remain true,
'Tis hard e'en for letters to cross th' bars strong.
All's wrong, wrong, wrong![3]

---

① The present poem constitutes a strong protest against the feudal convention. Though they had a happy marriage owing to their mutual love, Lu You and Tang Wan were compelled to separate because Lu's mother had a strong grudge against Tang Wan. A few years later, when they met at the Shens' Compound, the poet improvised this poem as an inscription on the wall to express his deep sorrow. The first stanza recalls the happiness and sorrow, and the second reinforces the poet's emotions.
② In the phrase "cruel separation", the adjective functions as a transferred epithet.
③ The repetition of "wrong", as does that of "grief" in the first stanza, gives emphasis to the word in question.

Relating Heartfelt Aspirations^①

◎ *Lu You*

For merits worthy of enfeoffment, alone on horseback I did go
Ten thousand *li* away to serve in the army in Liangzhou.
Passes and fortresses appear just in dreams, but when awake
I find my army coat tarnish'd by dust, which does thicker grow.

My hair has turned grey, and yet the woe
Is more aggressive: my tears in vain flow!
Who could have expected that one who aspires to fighting
In Tianshan should get older and older still in Cangzhou^②!

---

① In the present poem, the poet laments over the reality which allows him no chance to render service to his nation in times of danger.
② Here Tianshan and Cangzhou constitute two cases of metonymy, with Tianshan and Cangzhou respectively denoting the frontiers and a place where one is confined to a secluded life.

Immortals on the Magpie Bridge
Hearing the Cuckoos at Night[①]

◎ *Lu You*

In late spring th' winds and rains befall the rill.
'Round the thatch eaves and th' window — all is still;
Alas, the lamp is dim, and the night is so deep.
The orioles and swallows always silent keep,
But on moon-lit nights cuckoos will disturb my sleep.

Their plaintive voices will arouse the tear
Of th' lonely roamer — ere they disappear
Into the deep woods, — and break up their soothing dreams.
Hardly can men — e'en 'midst their native mounts and streams —
Endure their cries, let alone one who with grief teems!

---

① This *ci*-poem was written when General Wang Yan's staff office, with which the poet had worked, was
dismissed. It expresses the poet's loneliness in his tour from Nanzheng to Chengdu.

Immortals on the Magpie Bridge[1]

◎ *Lu You*

The fishing rod has witness'd sweats and pains;
Th' palm-coat has experience'd winds and rains.[2]
West to th' fishing terrace my home does lie.
I dread to near th' town's gate for fish-sales, as I'm shy.
Wherefore should I to worldly affairs myself tie?

When th' tide comes in, to hoist sail I prepare;
When th' tide's appeas'd, of mooring I take care;
And I return singing when th' tide is tame.
People tend to regard me and Yan Guang[3] as th' same,
When I'm a fisherman who makes light of a name.

---

[1] This poem pictures the leisurely life of the poet as a fisherman, who makes light of gain and fame.
[2] In this line the palm-coat is personified, and so is the case with the fishing rod in the previous line.
[3] Yan Guang (39 BC – AD 41), who had once and again rejected the emperor's offers of high-ranking positions, was a distinguished hermit of the Eastern Han Dynasty.

Immortals on the Magpie Bridge[1]

◎ *Lu You*

I'd gam'd in bright lights to my heart's content,
And on horseback strong bows I had oft bent.
That unconstrain'd life who remembers still?
Almost half of th' drunkards with their enfeoffments thrill,
While I alone become a fisherman on th' rill.

My little boat measures eight *chi* in length,
With three thatched awnings lacking in strength.
Yet it has to its own th' scenes of Pingzhou.
Th' Mirror Lake belongs to the free and low
From of old. What's th' need for th' throne his favour to show?

---

[1] This poem, by presenting the picturesque scenery, justifies the poet's preference of a fisherman's life to that of an official.

The Diviner
Ode to the Plum Flower[1]

◎　*Lu You*

By th' broken bridge beyond the post thou doth bloom
In solitude, expecting none to flatter.
At dusk the rains spatter, when thou suffer'st lonely gloom,
And the blasting winds do boom and thee shatter.

As with the favour'd in spring thou hast vi'd ne'er,
What matters if they should thee envy and blame?
Thou mayest wither, fall and be ground to dust, howe'er,
Thy fragrance will remain as before the same!

---

[1] In this poem, the poet extols the fine qualities of the plum tree: its noble loftiness in nature, its undaunted spirit in face of adversities and frustrations, and its unchangeable aspiration to better the world.

Charming Is Niannu
Composed at the Shihu Lake in the Same Rhyme Sequence with My
Friend's Poem[1]

◎ *Fan Chengda*[2]

The lake and th' hills rival paintings in charm!
I moor my boat by the willow-fring'd bank with care,
Thus the birds and fish I may not alarm.
Early spring chill, th' chance of blooming not all th' plants share,
With th' plums I may as well myself entertain.
A dream of three years since I went away,
During which of aging th' moon shows no sign
And th' same as before th' pines and winds remain!
My former neighbours salute me and say:
"At last you 're really home, for which we pine!"

New frost is added to what was raven hair;
Provided I can propose and reply toasts,
E'en if I'm nicknam'd "Senile Chap" I won't care.
Moreo'er, refin'd and tasteful riders come in hosts
To enjoy the isles and plants and rosy haze.
Unconstrain'd and ignorant of the ways
Of th' world, which I not the least treasure,
I take the bottle as my only pleasure:
As to he who hankers after wealth and fame,
Why should I deign to ask "What is his name"?

---

① In a natural style this *ci*-poem presents an idyllic picture of the poet's lakeside hometown and reflects the poet's lofty ideology.
② Fan Chengda (1126 – 1193), courtesy name Zhineng, ranks among the Four Greatest Poets of National Resurgence (the other three being You Mao, Yang Wanli and Lu You). His poetry, which is lively and realistic, reflects the daily life and sufferings of the common folk and condemns the evils of the oppressors.

Partridges in the Sky[①]

◎ *Fan Chengda*

The green and tender leaves are growing deeper in hue,
Here and there within the rails are seen buds red and new.
Atop the raspberry trellises th' bees buzz and hum;
Between rows of willows th' swallows deftly go and come.

I deplore my wandering life when spring wears away,
And resort to left-o'er wine and flowers to sane stay.
Oh! Wouldn't one more cup be nice for tomorrow's sake?
But lo! The moon arises in the setting sun's wake!

---

① This *ci*-poem, by drawing a vivid picture of country life, reflects the poet's love for nature, which is mixed up with a touch of sadness over the poet's wandering life. The masterly use of the verbal phrase "buzz and hum", being a case of onomatopoeia, adds much to the expressiveness.

Rinsing Yarn in the Brook[①]

◎ *Zhang Xiaoxiang*[②]

The waters of the lake melts with th' clear frosty sky;
The whips whiz and whir, th' embroider'd banners are red.
Thin mist and wither'd grass now and then catch my eye.

North to th' beacon our sacred land th' invaders tread.
At th' defence works out of th' east gate, I drink a cup
Of turbid wine, and 'gainst th' north wind sad tears I shed!

---

① This poem pictures the frontier life, condemns the crime committed by the aggressors and expresses the poet's deep sorrow over lost territories.
② Zhang Xiaoxiang (1137 – 1169), courtesy name Anguo, had held official positions at the Imperial Secretariat and in some local governments as the magistrates. As he advocated the recovering of lost territories, he had once and again received attacks and had twice been dismissed from office. He was a pioneer of the patriotic school. His poetry features a vigorous and free style.

Buddhist Dance
An Inscription on the Cliff of Zaokou in Jiangxi[①]

◎ *Xin Qiji*[②]

Below the Yugu Terrace th' Clear River gushes ahead,
Containing boundless bitter tears which refugees have shed!
I gaze into the northwest, where Chang'an lies,
But alas, ranges of mountains block my eyes.

The river, leaping and rolling, surges east,
By the mountains its current will ne'er be ceas'd.
Dusk falling on th' river, my heart sorrow fills,
When partridges are heard deep deep in the hills.

---

① This is a classic of the Xin School. It expresses the poet's great sympathy with the refugees, deep
sorrow over the lost territories and resolution to defeat the invaders. The gushing waters are
metaphors for tears as well as for unwavering determination, and the moaning partridges add to the
sorrow of the poet.
② Xin Qiji (1140 – 1207), courtesy name You'an and style name Jiaxuan, was representative of the Xin
School. Aspiring to delicate himself to the service of his nation, he plunged in the armed resistance
against the Jin aggressors when young. He had held several positions, including that of changé
d'afffaires of Hubei, Hunan, Jiangxi, Fujian and Zhedong. He had not only enriched the content and
expanded the realm of *ci*-poetry, but had also flied his own colors in style.

The Desk of Green Jade
The Lantern Festival[①]

◎ *Xin Qiji*

As if th' east wind sent down a thousand trees in bloom,
Which soon fall like hosts of shooting stars in full glare,
Fireworks of all sorts crack and boom.
With trails of scent, steeds and carv'd carriages along tear.
Soul-touching strains of flutes filling the air,
Painted gauze lanterns arousing delight,
"Fish" and "dragons" dance through the night.

With gold-trimm'd ornaments of unusual grace,
Shedding smiles and perfume, girls and ladies by pass.
A hundred times 'midst the crowds I've tri'd to him trace,
Yet when I chance to turn back, alas,
I spot him standing right in the place
Where sightseers and lanterns are sparse!

---

① This poem manifests that the poet is also a master in word painting. Such rhetorical devices as onomatopoeia (e.g. "crack and boom"), zeugma (e.g. "shedding smile and perfume"), simile (e.g. "like hosts of shooting stars"), etc., together with the surprise ending, make the description of the festival vivid.

The Moon over the West River
A Night Trip through the Yellow Sand Hills[①]

◎ *Xin Qiji*

The magpies flush out of th' branches in the minor light;
The breeze conveys th' chirring of cicadae at night.
The air fill'd with th' scent of rice flowers, I gladly hear
The frogs chorusing to herald a propitious year.

Some seven or eight stars the cloudy skies still reveal,
But two or three raindrops on this side of th' hill down steal.
I make a turn and hurry o'er th' bridge; to my delight,
A familiar inn near th' village temple comes in sight!

---

① Since he was ensnared by crafty sycophants and dismissed from office in 1181, the poet began to live a country life in Shangrao. The present poem mirrors part of that life.

The Joy of Lasting Acquaintanceship
Reflecting on Historical Events at Beigu Pavilion in Jingkou①

◎ *Xin Qiji*

Across this ancient land such great heroes
As Sun Quan are not to be found again;
The splendour of the great halls and stages
Has long been eroded by th' wind and rain.
Behold the trees and grass in th' dusk; 'tis said
That Jinu had liv'd in th' commonplace lane.
With a corps arm'd with sharp dagger-axes
And armour'd steeds, he shock'd th' land in his reign.

The hasty expedition in Yuanjia
Turn'd out the panick'd king's remorseful sore.
Fresh in my mind's Yangzhou being devour'd
Forty-three years ago by th' flames of war;
Whoe'er can bear to see Foli Temple
Bustling with pomposity any more?
Alas, but who would deign to ask Lian Po②:
"Is your appetite as good as before?"

---

① In this poem, allusions to historical figures and events are employed to express the poet's lamentation over the state affairs and keen longing for a drastic change in the situation.
② Lian Po was a famous general of the State of Zhao in the Warring States period. The king, who intended to reinstate him, sent an envoy to see if his appetite was still good (i.e., he was in good condition). As the envoy was not bribed, he gave the king the false information, "The old general went to the toilet thrice during a meal."

69

Fumbling for Fish

In the Year Jihai of the reign Chunxi, I was transferred from Hubei to Hunan. My colleague Wang Zhengzhi arranged a party in my honour at the pavilion on the hill, and I composed this piece for the occasion.[1]

◎ *Xin Qiji*

How much wind and rain is left of spring,
Which will in a hurry disappear?
Th' fallen petals come to me as a sting;
For love of th' season th' early blooming I oft fear.
"Oh, Spring! Please stay a while. It is said
That even th' end of the world is spread
With flowers, thus you'll find no path to tread."
Spring leaves without giving a reply, and within sight
Are spiders' webs catching willow catkins from morn till night.

Like th' empress's appointment in th' Changmen Event[2],
My rendezvous's cancel'd, for th' belles are jealous at heart.
Even if a thousand taels of gold could be spent
For Xiangru's *fu*, to whom can I my grievances impart?
Oh, don't be so complacent as to dance yet. Haven't you learn'd
Of th' much favor'd Yuhuan and Feiyan[3], who have both to dust turn'd?
Now lingering sorrow is the most consuming of all,
Thus for life's sake don't lean on th' railing of a tower tall,
'Cause th' setting sun's on th' lush willows casting its light,
Which constitutes the most heart-rending sight.

---

① Against his will to fight the invaders on the frontline, the poet was transferred to the Southern Jing-Hu Region as Deputy Commissioner of Revenue in the spring of 1179. This poem gives vent to the poet's indignation and disappointment.

② This alludes to the tale of the estranged Empress Chen who, hoping that Emperor Wudi of the Han Dynasty might have a change of heart, gave Sima Xiangru gold, requesting him to compose a piece of *fu* (an intricate literary form combining the elements of prose and verse) entitled *The Changmen Gate*.

③ Yang Yuhuan of the Tang Dynasty and Zhao Feiyan of the Han Dynasty were favored concubines of the monarchs.

Undermining the Battle Array
To Chen Tongfu to Convey My Encouragement[①]

◎ *Xin Qiji*

Tipsy, to watch my sabre I rais'd the wick of the lamp;
Awake, I heard bugle horns resounding from camp to camp.
Among th' battalions grill was portion'd out without delay;
Majestic martial airs th' band of fifty instruments did play.
Autumn saw th' warriors ready in battle array.

Our steeds were galloping as fast as the Dilu breed rare,
The arrows like stunning lightning were whizzing in the air,
I have been keenly longing to accomplish the wish of th' throne
For national sovereignty and become eternally known.
But lo, it is a pity that grey my hair has grown!

---

① This poem reflects the conflict between the poet's soaring aspiration to defend the nation and the indifferent reality, which are respectively signified by the grand spectacle of frontier life in the poet's mind and the grey hair. Chen Liang (courtesy name Tongfu), for whom the poem was composed, was the poet's close friend.

Celebrating Peace and Order
Country Life①

◎ *Xin Qiji*

Th' thatched hut low
And small verges on the brookside with grass green.
Th' grey-hair'd couple are talking o'er the cups, which does show
A strong Wu accent and an affection keen.

East of th' stream the eldest son is hoeing weed
For th' beans; th' second's braiding a coop of bamboo;
Th' youngest, lying upstream, is naughty indeed:
He's picking from a lotus-pod for a chew.

Hawthorns in the Wilderness
Touring Yuyan (the Dripping Cliff) Alone②

◎ *Xin Qiji*

My figure is in the limpid brook cast,
And on th' bottom is reflected the sky,
Where fleecy clouds are seen floating me past,
And I appear to be walking on high.

Who is singing in reply to my song?
A sweet melody comes from th' hollow vale.
Is it th' ghost? Or th' fariy? But both are wrong:
Th' peach trees in bloom a stream's gurgling to hail.

---

① The typical activities, related in a refreshingly simple style, imbue the present poem with a strong smack of country life.
② Here Nature seems to be animated by the poet's rich imagination.

Prelude to Melody of Flowing Waters

To Zhang Demao, Deputy Minister of Justice in the Capacity of
Out-going Envoy to the Enemy State[①]

◎ *Chen Liang*[②]

Do not think that in Northern Ji there is no steed,
Though the absence of Southern forces has been long.
The out-going official of mettle, for one, is indeed
More than a match for ten thousand men strong.
'Tis strange that dignified envoys of the Han breed
Should have submissively met the enemy's need.
Are they but waters in the rill, which towards the east trend?
But alas, to bow to th' yurts for th' moment just condescend:
We're sure to meet them in Gao Street and get back what we spend.

In Yao's land, Shun's domain and Yu's territories[③],
There must be one or two men of spine who won't sink
Into submission and cater to th' enemies.
On a myriad *li* of land sheep's smells now stink.
Where can the heroic spirit of our ancients be display'd again,
And when can we uphold justice and sovereignty regain?
Oh, just wait! Th' enemy will be put in a wretched plight,
For the sun of justice will sooner or later shine bright!

---

① Bursting with ardent love for the nation, great pride of the cultural heritage and full confidence in the final victory, the present poem stands out as a patriotic classic.
② Chen Liang (1143 – 1194), courtesy name Tongfu and style name Longchuan, was a prominent thinker, writer and poet of the Powerful and Free School.
③ Yao, Shun and Yu were wise ancient kings.

Charming Is Niannu

Ascending the Dominating Tower[①]

◎ *Chen Liang*

I gaze on high into the vast land,
Sighing over my strategy sound,
Which from of old few could understand.
'Tis strange that th' strategic vantage ground
Should have been deemed as bounds between!
What a place for striking out for peace:
The River of a thousand *li* it does face,
And it is back'd up by the mountains green.
Oh, it's incredible that th' petty household ease
Th' Six Dynasties should have taken with a good grace!

Thus th' Wang's and th' Xie's in scorn I hold,
Who atop the tower undue tears shed.
Th' stream's no excuse for inaction when woes untold
The folks suffer'd under the smelly nomads tread.
Just gallop ahead, when 'tis the right time to make
A long drive, without hesitation the least! Oh,
Be gallant like Zu Ti[②] who, to recover th' land,
Cross'd the stream, and our warriors will surely take
The initiative and defeat the foe!
For integrity we must get the upper hand!

---

① The present *ci*-poem expresses the poet's reflections on history and aspiration to recover lost territories. Allusions to historical events are employed to manifest the points.
② Zu Ti (266 – 321), a general in the Eastern Jin Dynasty.

Song of Yangzhou with a Slow Rhythm

On the summer solstice in the Year Bingshen during the reign Chunxi, I went past Weiyang. At the time the night rain had stopped and the buckwheat fields were boundless. Yet when I entered the city, what I found was a desolate town with streams running ruefully on their own, and the bugle horns began to whine when dusk fell. Feeling wretched at the contrast between the present and the past I composed this piece, which is regarded by Qianyan the senior as similar to *The Millet*.[1]

◎ *Jiang Kui*[2]

In th' great city south of th' Qinhuai,
Where th' Zhuxi Pavilion does lie,
I alight from the horseback for a brief stay.
What us'd to be a ten-*li* thriving way
Is now overgrown with all kinds of weeds.
Since to th' river come th' covetous foe's steeds,
E'en th' trees and desolate ponds may dread
Th' mention of th' flames of war, which had o'erspread
Th' land. In th' looted city, when dusk draws near,
Signal horns sound plaintive and drear.

Du Mu[3], who extolls the place in his verse,
Would be stunn'd if he were reviv'd, I deem;
And I'd defy his gifts to tell the grief o'er th' curse,
Though nice are his poems on reality and dream.
Oh, the twenty-four-arch'd bridge still lies there;
The waters shimmer in the silent glare
Of th' cold moon, and by th' bridge the peonies rare
Grow. Alas, I wonder for whom
The flowers from year to year bloom?

---

① The present poem, by making a sharp contrast between the pre-war prosperity and the post-war desolation of Weiyang (now Yangzhou), condemns the crimes committed by the aggressors. *The Millet*, which is mentioned in the introductory remarks, refers to a poem from *The Book of Poetry*.
② Jiang Kui (circa 1155 – circa 1221), courtesy name Yaozhang, was at the same time a poet, calligrapher, and musician. His poetry is marked with candidness and originality.
③ Du Mu (circa 803 – 852), a famous poet of the Tang Dynasty.

Urging Spring to Stay
Ode to the Plum Tree[①]

◎ *Shi Dazu*[②]

As thy lover I come to the brook to visit thee,
Intending to hang my endless thread of lovesick plight
On thy hazy twigs and moonlit branches. Oh, Plum Tree!
Whene'er the stream's shimmering with the moon's gentle light
In th' lonely evening, I cannot find a single place
To lay bare my feelings apart from this very site.

I have plighted myself to thee in the long long chase,
And now a keen yearning in my mind doth often wheel:
Be I at dream or at th' desk I long to thee embrace.
Who could have thought what I hear should turn out to be real?
The east wind, also easy in love, is stay'd by thee
Beyond the bamboos, as he can't resist thy appeal!

---

① What does the poet aim at, extolling the plum tree itself or expressing his grievance over his unreturned love? That is the question.
② Shi Dazu (1163 – circa 1220), courtesy name Bangqing, is known for his ingenuous depiction of objects.

Celebrating Peace and Order
Enjoying the Moon on the Night of the Fifteenth Day of the Fifth Month[1]

◎ *Liu Kezhuang*[2]

As winds swift and as waves fast,
To th' Toad's back[3] a myriad *li* I soar,
Where I made Chang'e's[4] acquaintance in th' past —
Though unroug'd, she's a beauty all adore.

Th' palaces of jewelry I tour in high glee;
Gazing down, the earth wrapp'd in clouds I find.
Tipsy, I casually shake th' Laurel Tree,
Which sends down what's term'd as breeze by th' mankind.

---

[1] This *ci*-poem conveys a sense of detachment from worldliness in a peculiar way. The rich imagination brings the poet to the moon, where stands the Laurel Tree and resides the beautiful goddess Chang'e in light of the Chinese mythology.
[2] Liu Kezhuang (1187 – 1269), courtesy name Qianfu, had held the position of Minister of Industries and Agriculture. His poetry features a free, powerful and romantic style.
[3] The three-legged toad is the metonymy for the moon.
[4] Chang'e is the goddess of the moon in Chinese mythology.

Congratulations to the Bridegroom

In Company of Lüzhai in Enjoying Plum Flowers at the Canglang Pavilion [1]

◎ *Wu Wenying* [2]

Tribute to th' hero [3] at his old abode we come to pay,
Where the glorious arbor does upright stand!
In Restoration an important role he did play:
If the east wind didn't grudge his fleet a helping hand,
He would have surely recover'd the lost land.
Dismissed, he lived in seclusion here;
Lo, the dew on th' branches seems to be sorrowful tear!
If th' Incarnate Crane [4] came to th' columns on a moon-lit night,
He would lament ov'er th' flowers and bamboos — a rueful sight!

We sightseers, who around the wise prefect throng,
Follow th' mossy path to see if th' plums are in bloom.
By the trees we intend to compose and chant a new song
So as the frozen buds and cold twigs to revive and boom.
In this regard I share with Sovereign of th' East [5] th' same will.
Things are worse today, and tomorrow will be worse still.
Facing the waters in the Canglang Rill,
None of us have anything to say,
We could only resort to wine and chase our gloom away.

---

① In this poem the poet cherishes his memory of the patriotic general Han Shizhong with a touch of pessimism. Allusions to historical events are employed to express the poet's sentiments.
② Wu Wenying (circa 1200 – circa 1260), courtesy name Junte, was an important poet of his times. He set store by form rather than by content.
③ This refers to Han Shizhong (1090 – 1151), a general renowned for his resistance against the Jin invasion.
④ This alludes to the tale that the immortal Ding Lingwei turns into a crane and returns to Liaodong.
⑤ In Chinese mythology, the Sovereign of the East is in charge of spring.

Green Are the Willow Twigs

My Thoughts and Feelings in Spring[①]

◎ *Liu Chenweng*[②]

Armour'd horses in blankets wrapp'd,
Silvery flowers shedding tear,
In the city of cares spring's trapped.
Th' flutes which are exotic to th' ear,
And the plays and drums in the street —
All are tragic to watch and hear.

Sitting lonely ere a temple lamp 'tis hard to bear,
Over th' moon-lit palace of a lost land I lament:
The ex-capital did once with splendor glare.
Although in th' mountains and sadness my days are spent,
The sentiments of Su Wu[③] in exile I share.

---

① In 1235, the mounted nomads came in the wake of the Jins to continue the invasion. The first stanza pictures the heart-rending sights of the enemy-occupied territories, and the second stanza airs the poet's lamentation over the situation and resolution to follow the shining example set by Su Wu — a heroic figure renowned for his unyielding integrity.

② Liu Chenweng (1232 – 1297), courtesy name Huimeng and style name Xuxi, was a distinguished literary critic and an important poet of the Powerful and Free School. He joined in the armed resistance against the nomadic aggressors, which was organized and headed by Wen Tianxiang. After the fall of the Song Dynasty, he lived a secluded life.

③ Su Wu (140 – 60 BC) had been sent by the Han Empire as an envoy to the Huns. He was held in custody and sent into exile. Despite the untold sufferings inflicted on him, his unyielding integrity remained unchanged.

Celebrating Peace and Order[1]

In the Same Rhyme Sequence with My Previous Piece

◎ *Zhou Mi*[2]

Th' tender warbler at dusk does wail;
Over th' lonely courtyard hangs a moon which appears pale.
Thick and fast fall the petals from th' peach tree like a storm
Of snow, and th' red bean[3] of lovesickness is taking form.

The ground is already cover'd with grass lush and green,
Whene'er will the wandering reins and saddle[4] return?
Oh, when free and easy my paramour could have been,
The floating catkins of poplars I unjustly spurn.

---

[1] The present *ci*-poem describes the keen yearning of a lady for her paramour.
[2] Zhou Mi (1232 – 1298) was a poet known for his exquisite style.
[3] The red bean is a symbol of love-sickness in Chinese literature.
[4] Reins and saddle: metonymy for "a wanderer".

Libation to the Moon over the Rill[1]

In Reply to Deng Guangjian in the Same Rhyme Sequence

◎ *Wen Tianxiang*[2]

Of all in the universe vast and wide,
The dragon[3], which is not to be confin'd
To the little pond, is the only pride.
In addition to deep grief on my mind,
Crickets chirp in th' cell, rains pour and winds blow.
Oh, th' ambitious Cao[4] who wrote a poem, spear in hand,
Turn'd into th' distress'd Wang[5] who, atop th' tower tall,
Compos'd *fu*, and then all th' efforts melted down like snow!
Howe'er, like waters in th' rill, in this land
More heroes are yet to come, after all.

As if a drifting leave I come to th' side
Of th' Qinhuai River again, at a time
When the north wind is puffed up with pride.

---

① Having been captured by the invaders, the poet was sent to Yanjing (now Beijing) via Jian'an (now Nanjing) under escort. The present *ci*-poem, written before the poet's departure from Jian'an, is of great spiritual momentum and sublime artistic attainment. The poet's utter royalty to his nation and indomitable spirit in face of dangers and death will forever shine with splendor.

② Wen Tianxiang (1236 – 1283), courtesy name Lüshan and style name Wenshan, was a renowned statesman, patriotic general and man of letters. When the Yuan troops crossed the Yangtze River, he organized armed resistance at the imperial edict in the position of Minister of Justice of the Jiangxi Region. Not long afterwards he was appointed Prime Minister and concurrently Minister of Defense. He fought courageously in Zhejiang, Fujian and Jiangxi before he was captured in the decisive campaign of Chaozhou. In spite of all kinds of coercion and cajolery to bring him into submission, he remained a man of moral integrity in the four long years of imprisonment, and was put to death by the Yuan rulers. Wen Tianxiang is a shining monument of patriotism and an immortal example for people of worth.

③ In Chinese folklore, the dragon is symbolic of sovereignty, magical power, or auspiciousness.

④ Cao Cao (155 – 220) was the ruler of Wei in the Three Kingdoms period. He launched an expedition against the kingdoms of Wu and Shu when he was Regent Prime Minister of the Han Dynasty. Before the famous Campaign of Chibi (the Red Cliff) broke out, he improvised *A Short Song* on deck the man-of-war.

⑤ Wang Can (177 – 217) wrote his *fu* entitled *Ascending the Tower* to express his homesickness and feelings about the sufferings inflicted by war and social upheavals while staying in Jingzhou as a refugee at the fall of the Han Dynasty.

In the mirror no more signs of my prime
Are left, yet royal the heart does remain.
On my way north to Longsha, I back turn
To see the lost territories that lie
Like a ribbon blue, which does lend me pain.
On th' tree at dim nights, friends who show concern
'Bout me might see th' Unyielding Cuckoo cry.